Mount Union College
Library

W9-AFV-379

Carnegie Public Library
219 East 4th St.
East Liverpool, OH 43920
(330) 385-2048

Waiting for the Sun

Carnegie Public Library
219 East 4th St.
East Liverpool, OH 43920
(330) 385-2048

Waiting *for the* Sun

Alison Lohans

Illustrated by
Marilyn Mets & Peter Ledwon

Red Deer Press

244386

Mollie's eyes blinked open. She could hear the tractor outside, like a giant bear singing. She bounced on her bed, then scurried to the window. Soon, the sun would come up. Every day, it popped up like a surprise and made her feel glad inside.

Out in the field, the tractor's headlights made pale puddles that slid along the ground. Dad was working, so that meant the baby hadn't come yet. Waiting for the baby was taking such a long time.

"Soon," Mom said, each time Mollie asked.

Mom came in and gave Mollie a good morning hug. Mollie snuggled against her mom.

"Will the baby come today?" she asked.

"I hope so." Mom put Mollie's hand on her big stomach.

Thump! A jab like a tiny hammer bumped against Mollie's fingertips. Something moved, then slid away.

"I felt it!" she whispered. She kept her hand there, but after that the baby held still.

Outside, the sky grew brighter. Mollie held her breath, waiting for the sun.

There it was! A burning bead bubbled up and grew. Then, suddenly, the whole sun shone red-gold over the farm. Mollie's eyelashes sparkled.

"Good morning, baby," she whispered to Mom's stomach.

It was hard to tell for absolutely sure, but just maybe there was a tiny answering wiggle. Out in the chicken yard, the rooster crowed good morning, too.

The baby didn't come that morning. Mollie's mom was tired and needed to rest. Dad went to town to buy chicken feed and a part for the tractor.

Mollie played outside. Meadowlarks sang. Dragonflies darted about. The breeze ruffled Mollie's hair and the old, dry cattails by the ditch. She caught five wriggly tadpoles in her jar. When the baby came, she would show it the tadpoles.

After lunch, while Dad fixed the tractor, Mollie made lemonade and took it outside. Her bare feet made a trail in the dust. Lemonade splashed cool on her toes.

Under the crabapple tree, she drew stick pictures in the dirt. Maybe she could show them to the baby. In the garden, she pulled fat green tomato worms off the plants and gave them to the chickens. The rooster called the hens with excited clucks. One hen laid an egg and shrieked, *"Cut-cut-cut—ka-DAHWW-kett!"* The baby would like the way the chickens talked.

Mollie went in the chicken yard and held the warm, moist egg in her hand. Laying an egg was sort of like having a baby.

The baby didn't come that afternoon, either.

That night, Mollie and her mom folded clothes that were waiting for the baby. Mollie laughed when Mom held up a tiny shirt that used to be hers. Later, Shirley the midwife phoned. When the baby started coming, Shirley would help. "Shirley helped when you were born," Mom said. But Mollie couldn't remember.

The next day, Mollie woke up late. After breakfast, she waded through the garden, where water ran in little ditches to the plants. She walked around in mud socks and got stung by a wasp. The baby didn't move when she waited so patiently, touching Mom's round stomach.

Grandma came to take her for an ice cream cone. Mollie yelled when Mom said she had to wash off the mud socks and change her clothes. The wasp sting hurt and itched. Grandma's car was hot, and the seat burned the backs of Mollie's legs. When they came home from town with a big pizza for supper and a stack of library books, the baby still hadn't come.

"Don't fret," said Grandma. "Just think, Mollie — someday you can read to the baby!"

Grandma stayed for the night. A thunderstorm
blew in. Scratching her wasp sting, Mollie
stood at the window smelling the rain, while
the curtains fluttered in her face. The tadpoles
swam faster every time thunder boomed. She
wondered if the baby would like the storm.

"Mollie," Grandma's voice whispered in her ear.

Mollie's eyes blinked open. It was dark. Somewhere, people were talking. She brushed a mosquito off her ear. Then she heard something else, a high, thin sound. She sat up straight. *"The baby?"*

Grandma smiled at her. "You have a new little brother — Benjamin."

Mollie nearly fell out of bed in her rush to get up. She ran down the hall, then tiptoed into Mom's and Dad's bedroom. Shirley the midwife was there. Mom was in bed. She looked tired and very happy. Beside her there was a wrapped-up bundle.

"Come, Mollie," said her dad. "Come see your new brother."

Mollie couldn't stop looking. The baby had a wrinkled, red face with eyes that were squeezed shut. "He's ugly!" she whispered.

Mom laughed. "Babies look ugly when they're brand new," she said.

Mollie remembered the first picture of herself.

But this baby was so little. She couldn't show it the tadpoles or the chickens or the dragonflies. She couldn't read to it. All this baby did was sleep.

A big lump filled Mollie's throat. She went to look out the window.

Grandma stood beside her. "Soon Benjamin will look much nicer," Grandma said. "One of these days, he'll be running around all over the place. You two will have such fun."

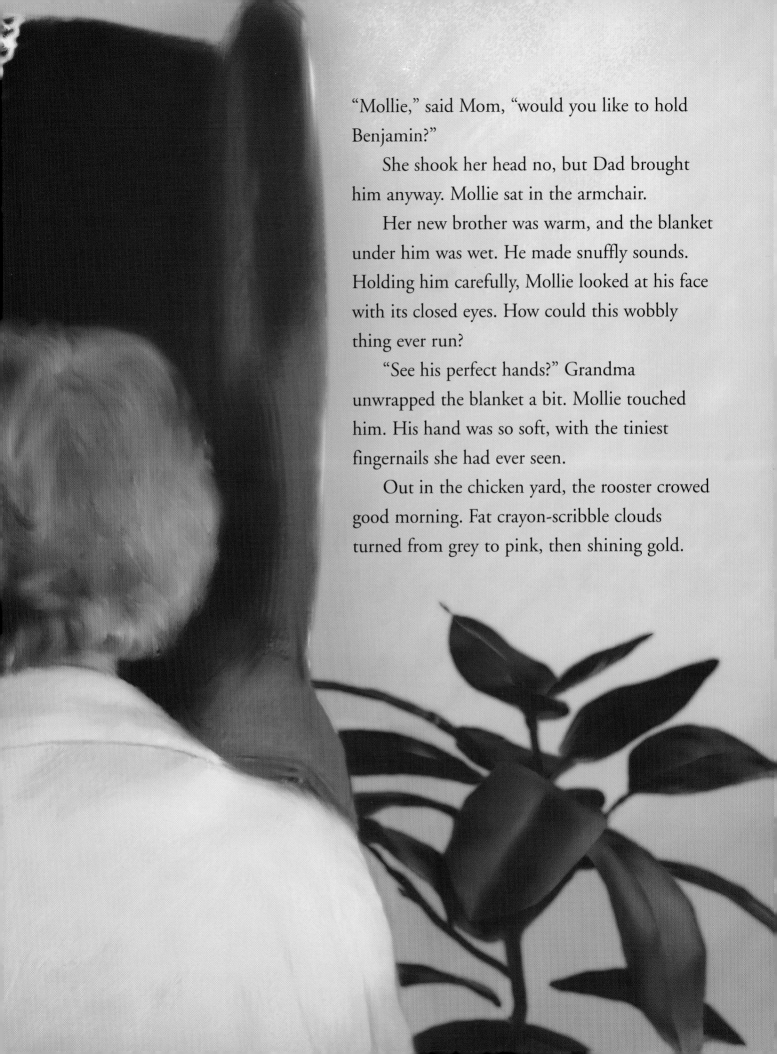

"Mollie," said Mom, "would you like to hold Benjamin?"

She shook her head no, but Dad brought him anyway. Mollie sat in the armchair.

Her new brother was warm, and the blanket under him was wet. He made snuffly sounds. Holding him carefully, Mollie looked at his face with its closed eyes. How could this wobbly thing ever run?

"See his perfect hands?" Grandma unwrapped the blanket a bit. Mollie touched him. His hand was so soft, with the tiniest fingernails she had ever seen.

Out in the chicken yard, the rooster crowed good morning. Fat crayon-scribble clouds turned from grey to pink, then shining gold.

In Mollie's lap, the baby made funny noises. His little arms wiggled. "What's wrong?" she asked.

Dad just laughed. "Benjamin is waking up," he said.

Benjamin's eyes popped open. He looked right at Mollie. Now he wasn't ugly, not at all.

Outside, the sky was very bright. "Look, Benjamin," Mollie whispered. "The sun's coming up."

And it was. A burning speck peeked up like a surprise, and soon the whole red-gold sun shone on Mollie and her new baby brother.

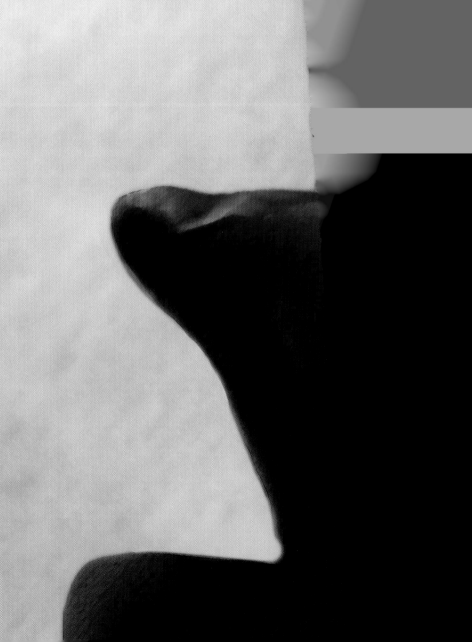

Someday, Mollie would show Benjamin the tadpoles. She would show him the chickens and the tractor. She would show him the tomato worms and the moon and the stars. Someday, she would read to him.

Today, they had waited for the sun.

Text Copyright © 2001 Alison Lohans
Illustrations Copyright © 2001 Marilyn Mets and Peter Ledwon
Published in the United States in 2002

All rights reserved. No part of this publication may be reproduced, stored in a retrieval system or transmitted, in any form or by any means, without the prior written permission of Red Deer Press or, in case of photocopying or other reprographic copying, a licence from CANCOPY (Canadian Copyright Licensing Agency), 1 Yonge Street, Suite 1900, Toronto, ON M5E 1E5, fax (416) 868-1621.

Northern Lights Books for Children are published by
Red Deer Press
813 MacKimmie Library Tower
2500 University Drive N.W.
Calgary Alberta Canada T2N 1N4

EASY READERS

Credits
Edited for the Press by Peter Carver
Cover and text design by Blair Kerrigan/Glyphics
Printed and bound in China for Red Deer Press

Acknowledgments
Financial support provided by the Canada Council, the Department of Canadian Heritage, the Alberta Foundation for the Arts, a beneficiary of the Lottery Fund of the Government of Alberta, and the University of Calgary.

THE CANADA COUNCIL | LE CONSEIL DES ARTS
FOR THE ARTS | DU CANADA
SINCE 1957 | DEPUIS 1957

ALBERTA Lotteries

The Alberta Foundation for the Arts

Alberta COMMUNITY DEVELOPMENT

COMMITTED TO THE DEVELOPMENT OF CULTURE AND THE ARTS

National Library of Canada Cataloguing in Publication Data
Lohans, Alison, 1949–
Waiting for the sun
(Northern lights books for children)
ISBN 0-88995-240-X
1. Childbirth—Fiction. I. Mets, Marilyn. II. Ledwon, Peter, 1951– III. Title. IV. Series.
PS8573.O36W35 2001   jC813'.54   C2001-910883-4
PZ7.L82893Wa 2001

5 4 3 2 1

For my parents, Walt and Mildred Lohans.
– Alison Lohans

For Aaron, Seth and Hannah.
– Marilyn Mets & Peter Ledwon

244386

Mount Union College Libraries

3 7048 00397 6020